Ghosts of Darke County II

A second collection of ghosts' stories

Rita Arnold

White Dog Books

ALSO BY RITA ARNOLD

Ghost of Darke County

Cover design by Ron D'Allessandris

ISBN# 0-9788463-5-4

To Mike and Susie
You always believed

Table of Contents

ACKNOWLEDGMENTS

A book of this type takes a great deal of help and assistance. Many people are involved in collecting the stories.

Again, I want to thank the Greenville Public Library. Not only is their book collection fantastic, but also the employees are extremely helpful. The genealogy room is wonderful for finding the old stories. Maybe someday the workers there will tell me about the unusual events that happened in that terrific old building.

I want to thank Rose Lambert, JoKay Miltenberger, Linda Riley, and Susie Weisenbarger for their encouragement to write this book.

I especially want to thank my husband Mike Arnold for his understanding as I spent time writing this book.

And a big thank you to all the people who shared their stories with me. And thanks to the people who were too shy to tell me the stories but they did mention when the event happened so that I could go do the research.

INTRODUCTION

Well, here we are again with more stories about noises and events that happen at night.

The response to the first 'Ghosts of Darke County' book has been wonderful. So many people told me how much they enjoyed the book. This was usually followed by the people telling of a 'ghostly' encounter of their own.

Many years ago when I started collecting ghost stories of this area, I never dreamed that I would be able to fill a file cabinet with them. Or that I would be writing a book; let alone two books.

Did these events really happen? To the people who told me the stories these were real events. I did not manufacture or invent any of these episodes. And for each story told to me, I would find other people in that part of the county to verify the story.

As in the first book, the names and locations have been changed. The people were kind enough to share their stories; but they wanted to keep their privacy.

None of these stories are told with the intent to scare or frighten. I only write this book to entertain.

As I go around the local area telling my stories to different groups, I am constantly amazed at how many people are interested in ghosts and ghostly events.

I wish you happy reading and hope that you enjoy this book.

1. The House

In Franklin Township there is a farm house that was built in the late 1800's, long before the invention of electricity, the telephone, or the building of modern highways. This farm has a large barn that at one time sheltered the horses, the equipment, the animal feed, and many other items needed to operate a self-sufficient farm. In addition there were many other outbuildings on the farm throughout the years for various needs.

To the west of the house for many years stood a small apple orchard. Also located near the house was a large garden which provided vegetables for the family and occasionally produces to sell for much needed cash. Behind the garden was a good size chicken coop. The eggs were taken to the local general store to sell or trade for items the family needed but could not grow or make themselves, such as sewing material, buttons, or shoes.

A short distance behind the house was a large woods. This area helped to provide firewood, building lumber, and a source of wild game that served as food for the family.

Like many homesteads from that time period, there were no close neighbors. People usually owned between 50 and 200 acres. This provided enough land for growing crops, raising livestock, planting a garden, and maybe a small orchard.

Over the years the farm was sold numerous times. Different families would move in to raise their children and enjoy the country life. Some families only stayed for a few months or years while other owners stayed for a number of years.

The current owners have completed extensive remodeling to the house and some of the outbuildings. The exterior walls of the house were not changed in any way. The bricks were cleaned and the mortar repaired as needed. Inside the home several walls were removed. The remaining walls were painted. New carpeting was added throughout the house, and new windows were installed. All the work was completed maintaining the original architectural details of the time period in which the house was built.

Recently the current owners of the farm have told me about their "interesting" company. As long as they have lived in the house, they have not been alone. No one has been harmed; but neither has anyone been totally alone.

When the family is all gathered in one room, it is common to hear heavy foot steps in different areas of the house. This is the sound of an adult walking through the rooms or down the hallway. No one is either seen, nor a white glow or mist, just the loud clear sound of someone walking.

When the residents got up in the morning after a night's rest, they often found that objects had been moved. A book was moved from the bookshelf to the table; a candy dish moved from the center of the table to the very edge of the table. A pillow was moved from one end of the couch to the other. But nothing was ever been broken. It appeared as if someone was rearranging the room.

While the children lived at home, the owners thought that the kids were playing tricks on them, trying to prove there was a resident ghost. But the children always denied having moved anything. The parents never made a big deal out of the events figuring there was no harm done.

As the years passed, the children moved out and had homes of their own. This left just the parents living in the house.

The footsteps continued to be heard. The objects continued to be moved around in the rooms. Still, each adult thought the other was playing games. They tried to laugh about the incidents.

Then one night, while the husband was away working the night shift, the wife was alone in the house. When she got up in the morning, the candy dish had been moved from one table to another. On a different evening she heard the heavy footsteps walking down the hallway. Now they knew the children were innocent. They really had a ghost in the house!

Are the builder and the first resident of the house still residing in his house? Or is one of the previous residents refusing to leave? And what does the ghost think of the changes to the house?

The current owners stated that they do not mind having a ghost. They never feel threatened by the noises. Nothing has ever been damaged. In fact, sometimes they enjoy having the company.

Rita Arnold

2. The Department Store

Jackson Township has a long history of being a fertile agricultural area where farmers raise corn wheat, soybeans, and various livestock.

This part of the county was settled by the white man in the early 1800's. Before that time the Indians roamed the land in search of wild game or just traveled the land following the seasons. The Indians did not believe in owning the land. They just lived off the land as needed to survive.

Throughout this area farms were claimed. The farmer's often left standing large wooded sections of land which provided areas for wild game to live. Sometimes settlers would form a town when a small cluster of homes was built where two streets would intersect.

On the western edge of the township is the town of Union City, incorporated in 1853. In its earliest times this town was referred to as a railroad center with various rail lines running through the town with the most recent line being the D G & U.

The town grew as it became known for producing building materials, vehicles, and agricultural products. In Union City's heyday, the trains would run through the town on the average of every 30 minutes or so day and night.

This is a town divided by the Ohio-Indiana state line. The main business area was developed in the mid to late 1800's on the Indiana side. These were usually wood framed one or two story buildings. A few of the businesses were built of locally made red bricks. The brick buildings were built with beautiful ornate work around the top of each building. The larger businesses such as the old opera house and the department store were large brick structures.

Beautiful houses of various sizes and design were built all around the town including on the Ohio side.

Ghosts of Darke County II

The department store that was built in the late 1800's was located on the corner of a busy intersection, one block north of the train tracks. In the front of this three story brick building were large walk-in display windows with wood floors. The two upper floors had numerous windows in front and on the south side of the building. The brick design is listed as "Italianate Commercial" by the National Register of Historic Places.[1]

The interior of this building contains a central staircase on the first floor with the old style wood railing that leads to the second floor. On the side of the stairway is decorative wood paneling. Located in the building is a large wood elevator that was used to transport the goods to the upper floors.

The second and third levels have wood floors that have the wear patterns and the creaks and groans of many years of continual use. On the second floor are arch ways in a wall that allowed the public access to the entire floor. Today a store would be built with smooth, even floors. But in this old building the floors are uneven with steps up and down to different levels on the same floor, giving the building lots of character.

For many, many years this was a very busy department store. People came here to shop for their needed house wares, furniture, clothing, and sometimes for a special gift to give to a loved one.

As time passed, people became more mobile. It was not unusual for them to drive longer distances to work as people began working off the farm. With the development of the shopping malls and discount stores, the towns' people would drive further for their shopping needs.

Unfortunately, business at the department store began to gradually decrease. Then, sadly, the store closed after many years of providing a service to the community. The community lost a good employer and a wonderful place to shop.

For several years the building stood empty. There were brief periods of time when a businessman would attempt to rehab the building; or someone would try to divide it into various uses, such as apartments or small shops. Nothing really worked.

Then in the early 1990's an antique mall opened on the first and second floors. Many dealers rent space to sell their items including furniture, china, and many different antiques.

The mall is staffed by paid workers and volunteers. Most of the employees have lived in the area their entire lives and remember the old department store from its glory days.

The mall is currently opened seven days a week. It used to be open late on Friday evenings.

Some of the workers have reported hearing unexplained noises. One person told me that they very clearly heard glass breaking; just like when you drop a drinking glass or a dinner plate. The employee walked all through the store and found that nothing had fallen off the shelves. There was no evidence that anything had fallen on the floor and broken. The only person in the store at this time was the worker.

Another person stated they would hear foot steps, the distinct sound of hard leather sole shoes hitting the floor; not the soft steps you hear with today's tennis shoes. Nor was this the sound of thin high heel shoes, but the loud sound of a hard heel hitting the floor as if someone were walking across the floor. The only person in the store at this time was the worker.

Also reported to me by an employee was the time voices were heard. This worker was cleaning the tops of the display cases when the voices were heard having a discussion, but not arguing. Not thinking anything was unusual, the worker just kept cleaning. After listening to the voices for what seemed like a few minutes, but probably was only a few seconds, the worker realized that no one else was in the building. Just to make sure, the worker walked through the entire store to verify that fact. Then the voices stopped. The only person in the store at this time was the employee.

Ghosts of Darke County II

The antique mall has a mannequin which is used in its display windows. Occasionally the mannequin is used elsewhere in the store, usually dressed to match the season or a holiday. But the problem was that sometimes people would bump into it causing it to fall onto a table or shelf. A few times a customer was startled by the mannequin thinking that it was a real person.

One day the worker arrived in the morning to open the store. As the worker walked around turning on the lights, it was noted the mannequin had been placed on the stairway landing between the first and second floors. Later in the day, the worker was talking on the telephone and mentioned that the mannequin looked good on the landing. It was out of the way and no one would bump into it.

That afternoon the worker heard a horrible, loud crash. Sure that something terrible had happened to some of the antiques, the worker carefully walked all around the first floor. But everything was found in place; nothing had fallen. Then, walking by the stairway, the worker found the mannequin lying on the bottom step! The only person in the store at this time was the worker.

Is this a case of employees from years gone by, still working at the store, but unhappy with the placement of the mannequin? Or were the voices and footsteps former shoppers?

No employee has ever been hurt or had a terrible scare. None of the antiques have been damaged. The employees just know that working in this grand old building includes hearing voices and footsteps.

3. The Library

During the 1800's, Darke County was being settled by people coming from the eastern part of America looking for a new and, hopefully, better life. They had dreams of good farm land at reasonable prices. Or maybe they had ideas of starting a business to supply general merchandise in the new territory. Or maybe they just dreamed of a new start in life.

As the communities began to grow in Darke County, the need for churches, stores, schools, and libraries developed. Families would gather and make plans for building a school for their children's education. Sometimes the school and church would be combined into one building. This would save the community time and expense that would be involved in building two separate buildings.

As time passed, the need or desire for a library would become apparent. Most of the communities could not afford to build a separate building just to house a library. Therefore a store owner would sometimes offer an empty room for this use, or maybe just a small section of his store. An unused upstairs room was often dedicated for library usage.

As the years went by, the collection of books would grow in number. Then some of the communities might be fortunate to be able to purchase an old house or an empty small building in town for use as a library, which could be less expense than building a new structure.

This was true for one small rural farming community in Darke County, a community where most of the citizens were farmers and had little money to spend.

In the mid 1900's one community was able to collect enough money from the citizens to purchase an old two story house. The citizens came together to support various fund raisers. The local businesses made generous donations.

This house was located on the edge of town on one of the main streets. Considering that the house was built in the late 1800's, this building was in remarkable condition.

Ghosts of Darke County II

A wealthy family had lived in this house for 50 to 60 years. Many children grew up in this house and played in the surrounding trees and land. Picture the children playing on rope swings, or enjoying ball games, or hide-and-seek.

As the years went by, the family either moved away from the area or passed on from this earth. The house then went through a series of owners. Finally it was purchased for use as a community library.

The house was set among a grove of mature trees which not only provided shade for the building but also made for a beautiful setting. There was enough land around the house to allow for parking and future expansion of the library as the community continued to grow.

As time went by, the library's book volume continued to grow until more space was needed. Eventually an addition was added to the building while the older section remained in use and also retained much of the original architecture.

The years passed and more space was needed. This time a larger more modern addition was added. Now the library could really spread apart the book shelves. This made it much easier for the staff and patrons to get around in the building.

The community was so proud of these improvements with more space for people to search for books, more shelves for increased inventory, and more tables and chairs for patron usage.

But, is someone unhappy with the old house being used as a library? Could a former resident or library employee be unhappy with the changes?

Most businesses have telephone extensions in several rooms. This is true in the library. Each extension has buttons across the bottom of the telephone that light up when someone is on that particular line in any room.

For years the staff had noticed that the telephone buttons would light up when no one was on the phone. In fact, no one would be in the room and a button would light up as if a line was in use.

There have been times when the first person to arrive at work in the morning would unlock the main door, then walk over to the counter. Here she would put her purse in the cabinet and glance around the counter for any notes left by the staff from the previous day.

Some days she would notice that one of the telephone line buttons was lit. Thinking that someone from the day before forgot to hang up an extension, she walked through the building checking all the phones.

Finding nothing amiss, she reported the finding to her boss who called the telephone company. The repairman arrived. He carefully checked all the extensions and found nothing wrong with the phones.

A few months later this event happened again. This time the telephone company sent out a different repairman. Again everything was found to be in good working order.

Then there were the times when calls would transfer to a speaker phone without anyone pressing a button on the phone. Again, the repairman came to the library, this time bringing his supervisor. Once again everything was found in good working order.

Now, after many years of the phone buttons lighting up and many different repairman not finding any problems, the staff has just become used to the lighted buttons.

Over the years the library has had many employees, most of whom were part-time workers, which allowed the library plenty of coverage when an employee wanted time off.

With this type of schedule, some employees would go a few weeks and not see each other. But when they did see one another, they found that they all have had similar experiences in the building.

The staff takes turns placing returned books on the shelves. There are times when the employees filing the books, knowing that they are the only people in that particular room, have unusual events happen to them.

As the staff is working, they feel someone pulling the back of their hair. The pull is strong enough to bend the head back. This can happen to female or male, people with long or short hair. The employee will feel a tug on their hair, then turn around and find no one else is in the room!

In a separate room is an area of the library for magazines and newspapers. Some employees have become very uneasy working in this location. (One employee told me that she refuses to go into that room). As they are returning periodicals to the shelves, others periodicals are being thrown onto the floor. The employees look around the room only to learn that they are alone.

The shelves are flat, not slanted. There is no way anything could fall to the floor without someone physically throwing them.

Many books are housed in one large room of the library which is very pleasant for the patrons to browse. One wall has large windows looking out over the lovely yard. There is the usual number of doorways, some for every day use and others for emergencies. Also there is access to the room by an elevator.

As with libraries of this size, there are times when the employee is the only person in the room. Or maybe not.

Occasionally an employee will look at the door way and see a man in a military uniform standing there. It is a faint, mist like appearance, but it is distinctly a gentleman in an old military uniform. It is a full dress uniform with a sword at his side. He makes no threatening moves, just stands there looking into the room.

Who he is no one is sure. He could be a former resident of the house. Or he could be a former employee just looking at the changes.

No one has ever been harmed by these unique events. But all the employees who have experienced these happenings realize that they are never truly alone in the library.

One employee told me that when the library is quiet in the evening, she finds comfort in knowing that she is not totally alone.

Rita Arnold

4. The Country Home

Does a house need to be old to be haunted? Can the sound of foot steps in the hallway or the hearing of voices when you are the only person in the house happen in a newly built house?

Located throughout Twin Township are numerous ranch style houses. Most were built between 1960 and the present day. These homes usually are near a road on one to five acres of land. The majority of these contain between 1200 and 2000 square feet of living space with either a crawl space or cement slab for a foundation.

A large number of the houses have brick exteriors and a one or two car garage. There may be a patio in the back and a small porch on the front welcoming visitors.

These are homes that were built on what was previously farm land in the early 1900's. And who knows, as the county was being developed in the 1800's, it could have been dense woods. Maybe at one time Indians traveled through this area.

There is one particular brick ranch home in this area that was built in the mid 1900's. After the home was first built, it had many different owners throughout the first ten to fifteen years.

The one family moved in and really loved this house. Even the children enjoyed living there. The house is now owned by the next generation of that family.

As with most houses, remodeling projects over the years have made the house suit the family needs as the time and space required.

But is someone or some thing not happy with the changes?

There are occasions when the owner will be in the house by herself while the children are in school. Sometimes she enjoys a quiet evening at home while the kids are with their friends. Is she really alone?

When looking down the hallway which leads to the bedrooms, sometimes she will see a misty, white glow. There will be no lights turned on in this area; and no way could this be a reflection from the sun.

Then there are the times in the evening, when the house is quiet, the children in bed, that she will hear footsteps in the hallway. No sound of doors opening or closing, just the distinct sound of footsteps. She checks on the children who are sound asleep. Knowing that she is the only adult in the house, she does become uneasy and carefully double checks all doors and windows. Everything was secure; and she found no strangers in the house.

Then there was the evening that her mother came to stay with her young son while the owner went out for the evening. As the boy walked down the hall to go to bed, he looked at the bedroom doorway, and suddenly shouted for his Grandma. The boy stated that there was a strange man standing in the doorway. The Grandmother saw nothing. After calming the boy down, she put him to bed for the night. The Grandmother figured the boy just had a vivid imagination and put the episode out of her mind. Who was this? Did he really see someone?

Then there was the night when the owner was alone sleeping in her bedroom. Suddenly, she heard teeth chattering in a dresser drawer! Slowly and carefully checking the dresser drawer, she found nothing but the usual clothing items she kept there. No one living in the house had false teeth, not even the play style false teeth.

After these events repeated themselves for a period of time, the owner decided to have the house blessed, hoping this would stop the strange happenings. The events did not stop completely; but they did occurred less often.

Is this the result of a previous owner or resident who does not want to leave? The owner stated that these events happened too often for it to be just her imagination.

Then one day the owner was talking to a sibling who lives in another county. The sibling happened to mention that they had a dream the night before that the land located next to this house in Darke County was formerly an Indian burial ground. The owner of the house gasped, she had the exact same dream on the exact same night.

Is the dream related to the mysterious events in the house?

I could not find any documentation about Indian burial grounds in that area. But who knows!

Rita Arnold

5. The New House

In some communities a housing development will occur when an investor buys acres of land, determines how large to make the lots, then places the streets and infrastructure.

In a rural area, housing growth can be a little different. Farm land that lines a township road occasionally is divided into about five acre tracts. This provides the opportunity for people to live in the country without buying a large farm. Also the original land owner makes some money. But the land is no longer being farmed.

In Harrison Township, along a quiet country road the land was divided and ten to fifteen new homes were built. Each house was different. There were even two log cabin style homes.

A young family living in an apartment decided after having their third child, that it was time to look for a house.

They did not have much money to spend; therefore they were not excited about house hunting. A handyman special or a fixer-upper would probably be all that was in their budget. After months of looking through the ads in the local newspaper, they were still in the small apartment.

The decision was made to talk with a realtor. The couple emphasized the budget situation to the realtor but also told about their dreams for more room. The realtor stated that he understood and would work within their budget.

Just a few days later, the realtor called the couple and stated that he found a house for them! And it was not a fixer-upper!

After hearing the realtor describe the property, they could not believe what they were hearing. The following weekend they went to look at the house.

They found a recently built (less then two years old) two story house on a basement. It had four bedrooms, a large kitchen and family room, five acres, and a huge two car garage. All within the budget. A dream come true!

The young couple kept asking the realtor why the house was priced so reasonably. You might even say "down right cheap." The realtor answered that he guessed the owner just wanted to move the house and get it off his hands.

The couple purchased the house. Soon they were moved in, enjoying the spacious rooms and the land after years in the apartment. They were so happy.

After just a few weeks, the wife noticed that unusual things were happening.

One evening, while her husband was at work and the children were all in bed, the wife was in the family room watching television. It was night time and the room lights were turned on. Suddenly the lights went off; and then after a few seconds they turned back on. She thought nothing of this happening, thinking someone hit a power pole somewhere. A few days later this event repeated itself.

This time she mentioned it to her husband when he returned home from work. They had an electrician check the house wiring. Everything was fine. Then they had the power company check their hook-up. Everything was fine.

The lights continued in this fashion as long as the family lived in this house.

During this same time period, the wife noticed the interior doors would open and close on their own. The children would be in school leaving the wife home alone. She would hang clothes in a closet and carefully shut the door. The next time she passed that same door, it was standing open!

The doors continued in this fashion as long as the family lived in this house.

The wife had read stories about ghosts; and how some people would talk to them. So one day she stood in the middle of the family room and said "we can live together with you, just do not cause any harm to us."

The family never felt threatened by any of these events. They knew this was just a part of owning that house that had an unseen resident.

Rita Arnold

6. The Building

Years ago a cement building for a service organization was constructed south of Greenville on the main highway in and out of town. This was a time when there were very few businesses or buildings of any type in this area. The building was surrounded by farm land with just a few businesses near by.

This organization (I have been asked not to reveal the name) was opened to men and women over the age of twenty-one. Unfortunately, after many years of service to the community, membership started to decline and eventually the organization disbanded.

While active, this group held many special events in their building. Dinners, dances, and family social gatherings were always well attended.

Also, the social room was often rented out to non-members for wedding receptions, anniversary celebrations, and graduation parties.

As Greenville continued to grow in population and size, soon the building was surrounded by other businesses. The highway was widened to carry increased traffic.

After years of being located in this building, the group could no longer afford to maintain the property or pay the taxes. They decided to rent a space in a different location of town and sell their building to raise some much needed money.

After the organization moved to their new location, the building stood empty and unused. Many months passed before the building was sold to a local business.

The new owners decided that the building just needed some minor repairs and painting. The structure of the building was found to be very sound. As time went by, the new owners noticed that the construction workers never worked alone except when working outside the building.

They only worked in pairs to do the interior repairs. In fact, the workers always entered the building in pairs. They would meet their partner outside and then go into the structure. But the contractors never complained about working in the building.

After the repairs, updating, and general sprucing up were completed, the owner moved his inventory into the renovated building.

One day, two employees went into the building to check on the inventory. Suddenly a loud piercing scream was heard! There was no radio or television in the building. After a careful search of the building, it was determined that they were the only occupants of the premises. The employees looked at each other and quickly left the building. They agreed to never tell any other workers what happened.

A few weeks later two other employees entered the building. While there, they heard distinct, loud footsteps. Checking the building they found that no one else was inside.

These employees quickly left the building, agreeing to never tell anyone what happened.

What caused these noises? Did some tragedy happen on these premises?

Old timers around town cannot recall any tragedy that happened in the building or near the building. No fires, no one became seriously ill, nor did any one die in the building. Nothing unusual ever seemed to have happened at that location. Maybe that is why so many happy special family events were held there.

Or, did something happen there that has been kept secret to the public? Will we ever know the cause of these sounds?

7. The Toddler

Are young children more sensitive to or more open mined about strange occurrences than adults? Sometimes I wonder if a child's mind might be more receptive than an adults' to witnessing a strange sighting.

A young couple early in their marriage lived in the old country home that the husband grew up in. This house was much like any other in southern Darke County. A two story brick home in the country surrounded by fields of crops and a small wooded area. A great location for the children to grow up, allowing them plenty of room to run and play games.

Occasionally the young daughter would wake up during the night and see a white misty figure in her bedroom near the foot of the bed. She would tell her parents about this in a casual manner, never acting afraid. In fact, she never asked to be moved to a different room or for anyone to spend the night with her. The child spoke about the ghost figure as someone would speak about an old friend.

After this went on for a period of time, the mother mentioned these events to a relative who had lived in this same house years before.

After some hesitation, the relative gave a detailed description of a white, misty figure that she saw years ago. She stated that the figure would stand by the bed much like a parent checking on a child during the night. The relative said that she never mentioned this before for fear people would think she was crazy or laugh at her. The mother could hardly talk for a couple of minutes. Then she stated that the description matched exactly what her child saw!

The relative reassured the mother not to worry. The ghost like figure was never scary or caused any harm to anyone. The relative found the misty figure a comfort when she was home alone.

8. The Passing

Is it possible for things to happen to us that are truly beyond our control? And the end result may be better then what we could have planned ourselves.

Mary currently lives on the old family farm. This is the place where she and her siblings grew up. It was a good life, playing in the barn, helping out in the fields, caring for the animals, enjoying church and school activities, and always having a loving family to share these experiences.

As the years went by, both parents passed away. The siblings married and moved to other parts of the county. But Mary remained on the farm. She kept some of the old furniture and household items from her childhood and added some new things of her own as the years went by.

In their later years, her parents had converted one of the bedrooms into a den. Here her father had placed a desk where he did the paperwork necessary for running a farm.

A few weeks after her father passed away, Mary was looking for an important piece of paper that she needed to settle the estate. She knew it could only be in this room, her father's den.

Her father never did his paperwork anywhere else in the house. After spending many frustrating hours looking for the paper and becoming discouraged, she yelled "where the heck is it?" Suddenly a gentle voice that sounded just like her father answered, "in the closet." Immediately she went to the closet. There on the top shelf was the much needed paper!

Months later as Mary was sorting through a closet in a bedroom, deciding what to keep and what to throw out, she found a baby gift that was intended for a boy. This item still had the store tags attached and was in a gift box ready to be wrapped. Mary then gasped for air!

Ghosts of Darke County II

Seeing this item, she remembered the old family story about her mother. Years ago, her mother had purchased a baby gift, came home, put it away and then could not find the item when she needed it. She even had the children help her search the house looking for the gift. Mary's mother laughed about this for years thinking she was getting forgetful. Eventually she forgot about the entire episode.

Mary set the gift aside and continued cleaning out the closet. Later that day Mary was to attend a baby shower for her nephew's new son. Was this her mother's way of sharing in the joy of a new baby in the family?

Could it be that even after death, Mary's parents are still watching over their children?

Mary said that these episodes never scared her. In fact, she was glad to know that she was not alone on the farm.

Rita Arnold

9. The Church

In Twin Township there are many churches of all shapes, sizes, and denominations. Most were constructed in the 1900's. A few of the really old church buildings were built in the 1800's.

This story concerns a church built in the mid 1800's. It is still using the original foundation. Over the years stained glass windows were added, an organ, then classrooms, and off street parking. Eventually the sanctuary was enlarged. Over the years members would occasionally discuss moving to a larger facility. But the talks never really became serious because no one wanted to leave the grand old building and the original location. This is a church that was built with lots of character and charm.

Like many churches, this church has changed denominations over the years.

Rita Arnold

In the back of the sanctuary on the wall over the last row of pews is an electric clock. This was placed so the pastor could easily watch the time.

The years went by, and the clock just kept running and running. Then one beautiful Sunday morning during the church service, a gentleman was sitting in the pew directly under the clock.

During the service he suddenly took a deep breath, grabbed his chest with both hands and fell to the floor. He was dead from a heart attack! The man had never been sick a day in his life.

A few days passed before anyone noticed that the clock had stopped keeping time. The pastor looked at the clock; then he looked a second time. This time he noticed that the clock had stopped at the exact minute that the parishioner died.

The clock was taken to a jewelry store for repairs. The repairman could not find anything wrong. He kept the clock for a few weeks. The entire time the clock was plugged into an outlet, it ran perfectly. He called the church to pick up their clock.

Within the week the clock was back in the church hanging up on the wall in the sanctuary.

For months the clock kept perfect time. Then one Sunday morning, the pastor, visibly shaken, noticed that the clock had stopped. It was one year ago to the day, hour, and minute that the church member had died. After this stoppage, none of the church members would sit in that spot under the clock.

The church, not having much money for repairs, decided to place the clock in the secretary's office.

Here the clock was plugged into an outlet. Immediately it started to run. After watching the clock run for a few days, it was decided to return the clock to the sanctuary wall.

After a few months the clock again stopped keeping time at the exact moment the gentleman died.

The electrical wiring was checked. Everything was as it should be. Tired of working on the clock, the church decided to buy a battery operated clock.

After a few months the new battery clock stopped keeping time at the exact moment the gentleman died.

Several years went by, and as sadly happens with time, the gentleman's dying in church faded from memory. Many of the older members either moved from the area or had passed away. New members joined the church; but they did not know the story of the gentleman and the clock.

On a beautiful Sunday morning during the church service, a lady suddenly stood up, took one step and then fainted. She was rushed to the local hospital to be checked by a doctor. A couple days later she was released from the hospital and returned home.

Ghosts of Darke County II

This lady was sitting in the pew under the clock. After the lady was removed, the pastor looked up at the clock and noticed that it had stopped running! One of the few remaining old time members walked up to the pastor and told him about the history of the clock. There was nothing wrong with the battery or the internal works of the clock.

Now the church makes no further attempts at fixing the wall clock. Instead, the clock hands sit right where they have stopped. New church members will offer to purchase a new clock but the church deacons always politely refuse.

Is this the gentleman's way of saying "Do not forget about me."?

Rita Arnold

10. The Farm

Did you hear that? A man in the kitchen just called out a lady's name, "Claire." "But I am the only person in the house," thought Anita. A careful search of the premises proves that Anita is the only one at home. But, who is Claire? And who called out her name?

In the 1960's Anita and her husband purchased an old run down farm house and the surrounding 300 acres. The house was built in the mid to late 1800's. Sadly the house had not been lived in for many years. The years of neglect were evident throughout the building. The wallpaper was peeling; and there was water damage on many of the walls. Many of the glass windows were broken by kids throwing rocks. Pigeons and bats were living in the attic.

Anita and her husband did not have much money; therefore they decided that this house would fit their budget. Over the years they would fix-up the property.

As time passed the house and out buildings began to show much improvement. They rewired and re-plumbed the entire house. Windows were either replaced or repaired. The floors were repaired where the wood had severe damage and then refinished. When the walls were down to the studs that is when the interesting events began.

Anita began collecting boxes of newly found personal pictures, old letters, school report cards, books, and even old clothing such as shoes, hats, and dresses. Some of these items were found in the walls; and others were found in the corner of the attic.

After careful study of these items, Anita was able to determine that in the past John and Claire Miller had lived in this house. Judging by the pictures and letters they occupied the property during the late 1800's and stayed until the 1920's or 1930's. Both Claire and John died on the farm and were buried in the town local cemetery. They had no children or close family; therefore the farm was sold at auction with the proceeds going to their church.

Ghosts of Darke County II

For the next several years the property went through a series of owners. At one time the house was a rental property; but no one stayed for any length of time. Eventually the house just stood empty. Soon the shrubs had grown higher then the windows, the paint began peeling, a few windows were broken, and the front porch sagged to one side. Inside the wall paper was peeling. There were some holes in the wood floors and some water damage evident on a couple of the walls. The attic even had a few residents such as birds, bats, and squirrels. A sad looking house. One that refused to give up and fall down.

Years after Anita and her husband had completed their remodeling of the house she decided it was time to study the treasures they had found during the process. Because of careful study of the old photos, Anita and her husband were able to return the house to its former glory. They even completed the landscape around the house just like the Millers.

Rita Arnold

Now Anita feels a kinship to John and Claire. When she hears Claire's name being called from the kitchen, she knows that it is John looking for his loving wife. In fact, she finds comfort in knowing that John and Claire are still enjoying the house.

11. The Business

When reading the history of Darke County, we readily remember the stories of clearing the land and developing the towns. But what happened when someone died?

When the settlers first came to this area there were no funeral homes. When a person died, the viewing and service were held in the home of the deceased.

Year's later undertakers built their houses with certain rooms set aside for funerals. The family would live in back of the building or on the second floor. As the years passed, some funeral homes were built as separate buildings. Even today some funeral homes are built with an apartment on the second floor.

No one is sure just when the custom changed; but sometime in the 1900's funeral directors lived in one area of a large house and kept public areas for the business. Could this make a house haunted?

On the edge of one of the smaller towns in Darke County is an old white wood framed house, built in the early 1900's. When the house was built the center of town was almost a half mile to the west. Now the town has grown and includes the house within the city limits.

There were train tracks behind the house until the late 1900's. Between the tracks and the house was a small creek. For a short period of time this home was used as a funeral home.

The current owners often wonder if this is the reason for the footsteps they hear in the front room some evenings. Occasionally they hear distant voices coming from that same room, as if a group of people were talking softly. They never hear laughter or shouting, just soft gentle talking. The sound of the front door opening and closing and the noise of dishes in use are all events that the family has grown accustom to hearing. Are these the sounds of funerals from long ago?

Ghosts of Darke County II

Or could these events be because the railroad tracks ran behind the house? Back in the days when hobos rode the rails, did they stop at this house for food or a day's work?

Rita Arnold

12. The Memorial Hall

Thanks to the generosity of Henry and Ella St. Clair, Darke County has a fantastic memorial hall, a beautiful place for an enjoyable evening of entertainment.

Henry and his wife Ella moved to Greenville in the late 1800s. There he became an extremely successful wholesale grocery operator. Not only was he an excellent businessman; but also Henry and his wife were active in the community donating their time and money to many causes.

Henry served on the city council, the school board, and was a strong supporter in the building of the Carnegie Library in Greenville.

For years Henry dreamed of constructing a hall or theater for entertainment and cultural purposes for the county. Unfortunately, Henry died before his dream could come true.

Ella St. Clair, like her husband, believed in the community and the need for arts and entertainment. She was determined to fulfill her husband's dream.

Henry St. Clair's will bequeathed money to the school board for the purpose of "erecting a Memorial Hall for the use and betterment of the public schools in any manner in which said board may think most practicable and beneficial to the public."[1]

After considering many locations around town, the school board decided the best location would be next to the library. The fact that the old high school stood on this property did not change their decision. The board decided to tear down the old school and build a new school in a different location.

Being unhappy about higher taxes, the citizens of Greenville defeated a school bond issue. The board then decided that the old school would be moved to the vacant lot next door. This would make room for the hall between the library and the school.

Ghosts of Darke County II

Once the school was moved, construction of Memorial Hall began in 1910. After two years of work, the Hall was dedicated in May, 1912.

The building was the beautiful result of true craftsmen of that era. But time took it toll and by the 1980's wear and usage had left the hall in sad repair. By the mid 1980's a restoration committee was formed; and the work of fund raising and building repairs began.

The public enters the hall through the front doors into a huge rotunda with a barrel type ceiling. The entire lobby is made from Vermont marble. The rest of the hall has been restored with attention paid to every detail.

Over the years thousands of people have enjoyed theatrical productions, lecturers, symphonies, community sing-along, school graduations and plays. Many traveling productions stopped here to provide an evening of enjoyment and entertainment for the citizens.

Rita Arnold

Many people have been employed by Memorial Hall as managers, stage hands, and custodians. Most of these people worked until they retired or moved on to other jobs. One long-time employee did not retire or move on. And sadly, over the years, the gentleman's name has been forgotten.

Years ago a man working as a custodian was high up on scaffolding changing light bulbs in the lobby.

It was near the end of the day; and he was in a hurry to finish working and go home. Just two more bulbs to change; and then he could go home. Tomorrow he would take down the scaffolding; but, tomorrow never came.

Instead of moving the scaffolding, he decided to stretch as far as he could over the edge of the scaffolding and reach for the last two light bulbs. He stretched too far and sadly fell to his death, dying instantly.

Did he leave Memorial Hall?

Workers and entertainers have reported sightings of a man who haunts the building. He has been spotted going up the stairs to the second floor carrying light bulbs in his hands. His footsteps are heard as he walks across the marble floor in the lobby, the sound of leather sole shoes on a hard surface.

Is he the one who opens doors when no one is seen near a door? Does he turn off the lights when no one is in the room? Is he the person who straightens up a room before employees return to work the next day?

Maybe some people enjoy their work so much that they never want to leave. Not even after they die.

Rita Arnold

13. The Road

In the early 1900's Darke County had many cemeteries dotted around the area. Because of traditions and due to poor travel conditions, people were buried in their local church yards or in the family cemetery located on their farms.

Remember, years ago cemeteries were regulated by a very few government laws.

Most of the people living on farms had small areas fenced off where their relatives could "rest in peace." The owners of the farms took pride in maintaining the family cemeteries. People would keep the grass cut, maintain the fences, and keep the tombstones in good repair.

In northwest Darke County along one of the older roadways is where one such family cemetery was located.

Sadly after many years of use, the family stopped burying relatives in their cemetery.

When people started to be buried in the larger city cemeteries or privately owned cemeteries, the small family cemeteries were no longer used.

As the years went by and the farms changed ownership, the family cemeteries became forgotten. The graves became over grown, the fences fell down, and soon the markers disappeared. Soon it became very difficult to see these cemeteries because all evidence of existence was gone.

This old roadway is just a narrow two lane country road. No lines are painted on the pavement, and very little traffic travels this way. The entire road is only about three miles long with no stop signs. The cross traffic stops. This road is fairly straight but rises and falls like a ribbon of candy.

For years nothing was located on this road except a few farms. Then in the mid 1900's some of the land along the road was divided into one acre lots and houses were built.

Ghosts of Darke County II

No one knows what happened to the cemetery or if the builder knew about the cemetery. Did he move the bodies to a different area? Or were the bodies already moved? Were the houses built around the cemetery unknowingly?

Many of the people living along this road have had strange events happen to them, mostly at night.

No one walks on this road at night. You might be visiting your neighbors in the evening; but you do not walk home. You drive home! And do not look in the rear view mirror!

Many people have reported walking this road at night when they hear footsteps behind them. They look back and see a dark figure following in the distance. If you start to walk faster, the dark figure will keep pace with you. Or if a person starts to run, the dark figure then appears in front of them. The dark figures will follow you all the way home. They do not go into the houses, just follow you home.

Rita Arnold

Are these dark figures trying to keep people from the old cemetery? Or are these the people who have been moved from their final resting place?

No one has ever been hurt, just chased and scared.

14. The Lady

Can a person die of a broken heart, or of loneliness?

In the early 1900's, newly weds Charles and Ruby Jones (names have been changed) moved to Arcanum to start a new life. They rented an apartment that was above a store in the center of town. Charles worked in the store that was downstairs. This was a wonderful arrangement for the couple because Charles could go home for lunch with his new wife.

Charles felt that life could not get any better. A good job and a beautiful wife. When he learned that a baby was on the way, he felt so proud and happy.

Then due to foreign events, a world war developed. Sadly, Charles felt it his duty to serve his country. After a tearful good-bye and a promise to return safe and sound, Charles left on the train to join the Army.

Rita Arnold

Ruby never knew such sadness. She missed her Charles so much. She stopped visiting with her friends because all she could think about was dear Charles. Friends became worried about her. But they agreed that once the baby was born Ruby would be just fine.

Soon a health baby boy was born to Ruby. She named the baby after Charles. All of Ruby's friends approved of this thinking that Charles Jr. would help to cheer Ruby.

But still Ruby remained sad and withdrawn. She would sit for hours in a rocking chair with the baby in her lap, looking out the window watching for Charles. She just knew that Charles would come walking up the street, back to her and the newborn baby. Then they would have happy times just like before the war.

But Charles never came home. He died in battle overseas and was buried where he fell.

Ghosts of Darke County II

Communications were very slow in the early 1900's. By the time the official word arrived, several days had passed. When the officer knocked on the door to notify Ruby, there was no answer. The police were summoned to open the door. After entering the apartment they found Ruby and her baby in the rocking chair by the window – both were dead.

The doctor, who had not seen Ruby for weeks, instantly noticed how thin she was. After checking Ruby and the baby over, the doctor stated that they died of dehydration and malnutrition.

Did she die of loneliness waiting for Charles to return? Or did she die of a broken heart?

Over the years the store changed ownership and businesses many times. For a few years the store and apartment stood empty. The apartment had been used as a storage area for forty to fifty years.

Rita Arnold

Then the store became an antique store which used both floors for display. By removal of the door from the stairway, that made the old apartment easily accessible to the public.

Since removing the door, the store owner noticed a nice breeze coming down the stairs. But occasionally the store owner heard a door shut at the stairway but the door is gone! And then she no longer felt the breeze.

Customers, who know nothing about the history of the store, come down from the second floor commenting about the lady in the rocking chair near the window wearing clothing from the early 1900's. The lady is holding a baby.

Is Ruby still waiting for Charles to come home?

15. The Park

Can a town park be haunted? Oh yes, without a doubt! Especially if the park area is in an older section of town near where the railroad tracks were once located. Then throw in a nice size creek, a wooded area, and plenty of tall trees. Sounds like a prefect setting for some ghostly happenings.

The Arcanum Park has an interesting history. In the last half of the 1800's the Ivester family built a beautiful two story brick house on property located on the north edge of town (at that time). Behind the house, towards the north, was a large wooded area with a creek and plenty of grassy area for walking and playing.

The Ivester children grew and some of them moved away. One married daughter remained in the house. When she passed away in the 1920's, she willed this land to the village as a park. The home was then sold at an auction.

As the years went by, the railroads were laying tracks throughout Darke County. Soon the railroad gained the right of way to lay tracks near the creek in the park and on through town. In the center of town was located the local train depot.

The train tracks are now gone. But despite being overgrown with trees and shrubs, the land still shows some evidence of once having been a railroad right of way. Some of the old track bed makes for a nice shaded walking area. But be careful of whom you meet along the way or what you see.

There are times when walking through the park near the creek bed you think you see a man lying there on the ground. You step back, take a closer look and realize that your eyes are playing tricks on you. Or are they?

There is a story around town that in the early 1900's, there was a train wreck near what is now Ivester park. Maybe some of the cars jumped the tracks and landed in the creek. Could this sighting be someone who died as a result of this wreck?

The other story is about a young male high school student in the park. Years ago there was an old football field near the park. Unfortunately, a football player died on this field in an accident while playing football. No one remembers the circumstances surrounding the death. In recent years people have reported seeing a vision of a young man in the park lying on the ground. Could it be that the player is still around?

No one has ever reported being chased or harmed by the sighting; just that they see a man one second and the next he is gone from sight. And he is always spotted lying on the ground as if injured or dead.

Rita Arnold

16. The Train

I hear that train a comin';
It's rollin' 'round the bend.

-John R. Cash

Hear we are, headed for home late at night, just west of Bradford, near the old Ballinger Run Creek. The fog is extremely dense and if we are not careful, we will miss our turn onto Zerber Road. Listen! A train is coming!

How can that be? The tracks were abandoned and removed years ago! Oh no, it's the ghost train!

Bradford, Ohio, for over one hundred and thirty years was a railroad town. A town where two train lines met, home to a roundhouse that provided a service area for the locomotives, a mecca for new families seeking jobs and a better living for their families.

As the train traffic increased so did the town size. More houses, schools, churches, and businesses were built. Then in 1929 the terminal was closed; and the railroad employment started to dwindle.

In the early years of railroading, train wrecks would happen frequently. But as the technology and building materials improved, the wrecks became less frequent. Safety became an important concern for the railroad companies.

Then, on May 21, 1939, an incident occurred that would become known as the great train wreck.

It all started in Logansport, Indiana, where three freight trains left the station about 45 minutes apart, all headed for Columbus, Ohio. These were daily runs, nothing new or unusual for the conductors. All three trains departed the station between 10:40PM and 12:30AM. The trains were a good size, 84 cars, 54 cars, and 85 cars long, respectively. Each train was carrying produce, lettuce, potatoes, processed food, and livestock such as cattle and hogs. All this cargo was normal for the trains of the era.

Ghosts of Darke County II

The weather was clear when the trains started their runs. Then a fog developed which became heavier as the trains proceeded east with visibility reported at less then four hundred feet as the trains approached Union City, Indiana.

About eighty miles west of Union City, Indiana, the second train saw the rear of the first train which was about one and a half mile distant. The second train then decreased its speed to about eighteen miles per hour. Also, the second train had spotted a burned out fusee (a red signal flare used especially for protecting stalled trains and trucks). The train carefully continued eastward.

As the second train approached Woodington, Ohio, (Darke County), it was flagged down and stopped about forty car lengths behind the first train.

After a short period of time the first train departed with the second train following at an appropriate distance. As the trains proceeded east, the second train was traveling at approximately twenty-eight miles per hour.

Rita Arnold

The weather had cleared and the conductor had an unrestricted view of about one mile. But suddenly, a very dense fog developed and completely wrapped around the trains. The second train had just entered the fog, about fifty feet or so when the conductor saw the caboose of the first train stopped about three car lengths ahead! The train continued eastward unable to stop.

Unknown to the second train, the first train had stopped at 2:13AM leaving the cars and caboose on the tracks just west of Ballinger Run Calvert (now called Ballinger Run Creek). The engines went on to the coal dock. Remember, during this time period, communication was only by means of flares and lanterns.

The second train collided with the first train for the first collision. The second train ripped through the caboose and a car. Plus it knocked the next six cars off the track. Many local citizens heard the crash and came to aid in the rescue.

Ghosts of Darke County II

At the same time, the third train had just passed the Union City tower moving at a high rate of speed. The conductor had orders to pass the previous two trains.

About 120 car lengths west of the wreck, fusees were placed and a flagman was positioned to flag down the third train. As the third train approached, the flagman signaled the train to stop, but the train passed him traveling about 60 to 65 miles per hour. The engineer stated that he saw the signal but thought the signal was for west bound trains. The train fireman also saw the signal but thought it was not important. The train continued eastward.

Near the collision sight, the second train conductor signaled the third train to stop. Again the train fireman saw the signal; but this time thought this signal was a greeting light and signaled back.

The third train then ran into the wreckage! From Zerber Road to Ballinger Run Creek were train cars on their sides; engines were upside down. The cars were splintered and twisted pieces of metal destined for repair or more likely the junkyard.

More and more the local citizens came to the crash sight bringing their lanterns with them, wanting to help. Both railroad employees and citizens worked to aid the injured. With the use of primitive tools and their bare hands, the dead and injured were pulled from the wreckage.

As dawn broke over the eastern horizon, the total was four crewmen dead and four more were injured and taken to the local hospital. Additionally, there was a large number of livestock on the ground lying dead or severely injured. The cry of the people and animals was something that the rescuers would never forget.

Years ago these tracks were abandoned by the railroad company. Then after a few years the tracks were removed and the land was sold. Some areas were purchased by neighboring farmers who then enlarged their fields. Other areas of old track bed are now used by private companies; and still other areas are used as trails for hiking and biking.

Ghosts of Darke County II

But are they truly abandoned? People in recent years have reported hearing the cries for help and the loud moans and cries of animals in great pain. When citizens talk about hearing the cries, they noticed two common facts. One, that the sounds occur on a dense foggy night; and two, the cries are heard in the month of May.

Was the suffering so great that the injured are still calling for help?

And is this the reason that on a still night you can hear a train whistle?

Notes

The Department Store
Wilson, Frazer, *"Darke County, Ohio"* P 548-9

The Library
Miltenberger, JoKay, Hill, JoAnne, *"Arcanum, A Secret Place"* P 51-53

The Memorial Hall
Thieme, Jean Louise; Shultz, Mary Francis; Feltman, Roberta; Longfellow, Elaine, Kensinger, Richard; *"The Henry St. Clair Memorial Hall Restoration"* P 1-3

The Park
"Is Arcanum Public Library Haunted?" *The Daily Advocate,"* (October 15, 2002)

The Train
Trostel, Scott D. *"Bradford the Railroad Town"* 1987

Once upon a midnight dreary
While I pondered, weak and weary.

Over many a quaint and curious volumne of forgotten lore-
While I nodded nearly napping, suddenly there came a
tapping,
As of some one gently rapping, rapping at my chamber door.

"The Raven"   Edgar Allen Poe

_____

www.ingramcontent.com/pod-product-compliance
Lightning Source LLC
Chambersburg PA
CBHW020621130626
46552CB00003B/1070